For fans of the Carolina Tales Series

. . .

. . . *Beginnings - The Sullivan's Island Supper Club* is a collection of scenes that explore how Tallulah Wentworth and Eugenia Ladson met Quinn Poinsett, Libba Graham, and Sarabeth Boone, and how the ladies, along with Birdie Markley and Camille Houston became *The Sullivan's Island Supper Club*.

These are scenes cut from the novel, *The Sullivan's Island Supper Club*, and offered for readers who would like more background on the characters who appear in the *Carolina Tales*. If you've never read one of the *Carolina Tales*, I would encourage you to start with either *The Sullivan's Island Supper Club* or *Big Trouble on Sullivan's Island* and come back to these additional scenes later. I believe these will be most enjoyed by readers who are familiar with the characters and setting. I so hope you enjoy these glimpses into the formation of the supper club!

Beginnings – The Sullivan's Island Supper Club

Sunsplashed Southern Stories
BY SUSAN M. BOYER

Carolina Tales Series

Big Trouble on Sullivan's Island

Beginnings - The Sullivan's Island Supper Club (Prequel)

The Sullivan's Island Supper Club

Trouble's Turn to Lose (April 8, 2025)

Hard Candy Christmas (October 28, 2025)

The Liz Talbot Series

Lowcountry Boil (A Liz Talbot Mystery # 1)

Lowcountry Bombshell (A Liz Talbot Mystery # 2)

Lowcountry Boneyard (A Liz Talbot Mystery # 3)

Postcards From Stella Maris (Five Liz Talbot Short Stories)

Lowcountry Bordello (A Liz Talbot Mystery # 4)

Lowcountry Book Club (A Liz Talbot Mystery # 5)

Lowcountry Bonfire (A Liz Talbot Mystery # 6)

Lowcountry Bookshop (A Liz Talbot Mystery # 7)

Lowcountry Boomerang (A Liz Talbot Mystery # 8)

Lowcountry Boondoggle (A Liz Talbot Mystery # 9)

Lowcountry Boughs of Holly (A Liz Talbot Mystery # 10)

Lowcountry Getaway (A Liz Talbot Mystery # 11)

Beginnings - The Sullivan's Island Supper Club

A CAROLINA TALE

SUSAN M. BOYER

STELLA MARIS BOOKS
LLC

Beginnings - The Sullivan's Island Supper Club

A Carolina Tale

First Edition | August 2024

Stella Maris Books, LLC

5052 Old Buncombe Road, Suite A-273

Greenville SC 29617

https://stellamarisbooksllc.com

Cover Artwork © 2023 by Marina Kaya, Qamber Designs, used by exclusive license

Cover design by Elizabeth Mackey

Author photograph by Mic Smith

ISBN 978-1-959023-34-0 (E-book)

ISBN 978-1-959023-35-7 (Paperback)

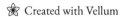 Created with Vellum

For my readers who like to know the whole story...

About These Scenes

These are scenes cut from the novel, *The Sullivan's Island Supper Club*. I'm making them available for readers who would like more background on the characters who appear in the *Carolina Tales*.

If you've never read one of the *Carolina Tales*, I would encourage you to start with either *The Sullivan's Island Supper Club* or *Big Trouble on Sullivan's Island* and come back to these additional scenes later.

I believe these will be most enjoyed by readers who are familiar with the characters and setting. I wrote the scenes as I was developing the characters' backgrounds.

I so hope you enjoy these glimpses into the formation of the supper club!

Warmly,

Susan M. Boyer

Tallulah Meets Quinn

Chapter One

April 9, 2017 1:00 p.m.
The Obstinate Daughter
Sullivan's Island, South Carolina
Tallulah Wentworth

The Obstinate Daughter was Tallulah's favorite restaurant on Sullivan's Island, maybe in the entire Lowcountry. She was certain that's why Eugenia had somehow wrangled a reservation, though they were notoriously hard to come by last minute. Eugenia could be relentless. Tallulah had personally never met anyone who'd successfully said no to Eugenia Beatriz Butler Ladson. So, there they were, in Tallulah's favorite booth by the window, enjoying lunch after church. Eugenia hadn't even argued, had gone with her without objection to Holy Cross, when Tallulah knew for a fact Eugenia had been visiting that non-denominational church with Fish. Fish was conspicuously absent today, which could only mean that Eugenia meant to focus on Tallulah like a brain surgeon removing an aneurysm.

"I've always hated beets," said Tallulah. "I think they must do something sinful to these. They're delicious. Must be sorcery."

SUSAN M. BOYER

She put another bite of beets, cheese, and sauce together and delivered it to her mouth.

"Have you given any further thought to something you might like to get involved in?" asked Eugenia. "A new project?"

Tallulah sighed a long-suffering sigh. "How do I unsubscribe as *your* new project? Where do you suppose you get this? This burning desire to fix people. Some of us can't be fixed you know."

"I'm not sure. It's a character flaw, of course. Perhaps after we deal with your issues I'll see a therapist or a holy man."

"There's no dealing with my issues, as you put it," said Tallulah. "Henry's dead. You can't bring him back, can you?"

"Aren't you afraid you have unfinished business?"

Tallulah screwed up her face. "Like what, for example?"

Eugenia shrugged. "That's not for me to say. What's something you tried to get Henry to do, but he wouldn't? There must be something. Men can be so stubborn."

"Well, he wouldn't eat Brussels sprouts..."

Eugenia closed her eyes and inhaled a long, slow breath. "Perhaps there's something else."

"I'll let you know if I think of anything. Are you going to finish those polenta fries?"

"Help yourself," said Eugenia. "Seriously, Tallulah, how are you feeling today?"

"I'm fine," said Tallulah, "except for the fact that my life is over."

"Clearly it's not," said Eugenia. "Here you sit. We just need to figure out something for you to do with it."

"Want to share a piece of lemon cake?"

"Sure, why not? Food is a start. As a reason to live, it's quite limited, I think you'll find. And you might want to take up an exercise program as well."

2

Chapter Two

Meanwhile, in the parking lot...
April 9, 2017 2:00 p.m.
The Obstinate Daughter
Sullivan's Island, South Carolina
Kathleen Quinn O'Leary Poinsett

They were going to be late for their reservation, Quinn just knew
it. Anxiety gnawed at her stomach. It was such a familiar sensa-
tion, she sometimes didn't even notice, had to stop to think about
what she was anxious about. Occasionally, she couldn't think of a
thing. She'd just practice her focused breathing and concentrate
on making her stomach muscles relax. This wasn't one of those
times. She knew exactly what was causing her heart to race and
her jaw muscles to tense: her parents.

You'd think they would've matured enough at this stage of the
game to stop with all the bickering, the melodramatic arguments.
Her father was sixty-eight years old for goodness sake, her mother
only two years younger. Their relationship had always been
tumultuous, their grand passion the center of their universe.
Quinn was accustomed to being a bit player in their sweeping
drama. Why couldn't they putter in the garden like normal grand-

parents? No, hang gliding, parasailing, and *knife throwing*...these were the hobbies her parents had dabbled in recently.

Quinn turned on the auxiliary power and rolled down the windows on the ridiculously large Lexus SUV Redmond had bought her. She did need the third row of seating. She couldn't argue the point. And yes, she wanted Oliver and the twins to be safe, of course she did. It wouldn't be long before the twins wouldn't want to ride around with her at all—they'd be twelve in October, and Quinn knew all bets were off once they were teenagers.

Where had the time gone? It seemed like only yesterday she and Redmond had gotten married, and the twins were three years old. Shepherd and Sutton were the most adorable toddlers. It was such a sad story...their mother had died giving birth. She'd had preeclampsia, which had caused high blood pressure. Then there were complications and emergency surgery to stop the bleeding, but of course they didn't—not in time. And poor Redmond was grieving and trying to raise twins by himself. Well, he had help, of course he did—he had to. He was a doctor, an anesthesiologist. He couldn't very well quit work and stay home with the babies. Someone had to provide for them. But things had worked out beautifully. Quinn had said countless times, to everyone she knew, that she couldn't love those kids more if she'd given birth to them. And she had honestly believed that, right up until Oliver was born five years later.

She didn't love Shepherd or Sutton any less—perish the thought. But if she was honest with herself, she had to admit there was something special—something biological, not something she could possibly help—about her connection to Oliver. Were the twins jealous of him? She sometimes wondered, but she really didn't think so. They were so busy with their own lives—so much older. Oliver was only two—he'd be three in July. Shepherd was busy with golf, and Sutton with cheerleading and her friends. It was a wonder they'd had time to notice they had a little brother at all. But they were really good with Oliver and he idolized them.

Ten after. Quinn sighed and tried calling her mother again.

"I'm on my way!" Myrna said when she picked up the phone on the fourth ring.

"Mamma, we're late. They've probably already given our table away. Where are you?"

"Well, I—"

"Come back to bed, my goddess." Quinn's father called.

"Oooh! Really, Mamma?" At least they weren't fighting again.

"Finn, stop that." Myrna giggled. "Quinn, I'll be right there. You want to go ahead and order for us? I'm thinking I'll have the—"

"No, no. I'll just wait for you in the car."

Her mother gave a pained little sigh. "Fine. Give me ten minutes."

"Love you, Katie Quinn," her father called just before her mother ended the call.

Quinn closed her eyes, took a deep breath, and let it out slowly. Why didn't she have siblings she could commiserate with? When she opened her eyes, Libba Graham and her three kids were approaching the parking lot in a golf cart. While Libba waited for traffic to clear so she could turn in, Quinn hit the auxiliary power and rolled up the car windows. She didn't want to get drawn into a chat about why she was sitting in the parking lot. Libba might be the chattiest person Quinn knew, and her oldest, Mia, was only a year behind the twins in school. Quinn was careful not to do anything that would cause comment, maybe embarrass Shepherd and Sutton, or worse still, Redmond. His first wife's family had deep roots in Charleston, and firm ideas about decorum. They were very involved grandparents, not that that was a bad thing. Maybe she should just drive around the block and come back when her mother arrived.

She started the car, put it in reverse, and backed out of the parking space. Quinn glanced from the screen, where the backup camera showed what was directly behind her, to the sideview mirror, then, out of habit to the rearview mirror.

That's when she noticed the gigantic wasp on the ceiling.

She sucked in her breath and scrunched down.

Surreptitiously, she reached for the button to lower the windows.

The wasp flew straight at her with purpose.

Ohmygosh. Ohmygosh. Ohmygosh. Quinn batted the air in front of her with one hand and fumbled with the door with the other. She scrambled out of the car and lunged around the door, landing in the dirt and gravel parking lot just as the Lexus slammed into the silver Mercedes S-Class.

Chapter Three

A few seconds earlier...
Parking lot at The Obstinate Daughter
Sullivan's Island, South Carolina
Tallulah Wentworth

"I was thinking we'd run by and see Birdie for a few minutes." Eugenia put the car in reverse and eased out of the parking space.

"Drop me off at home first, would you?"

"Oh, I'm not nearly up to being out by myself yet. I'm still not feeling up to par to be honest. That last round of chemotherapy was brutal. I've probably overdone it today. I hate to ask, but I really need to stay with you a while longer."

Tallulah lifted an eyebrow at her friend.

"What?" Carefully looking in all directions, Eugenia shifted the car into drive and rolled forward.

"This is the first you've mentioned feeling poorly today. And yet you want to make a social call. I know full well what you're up to."

"I have no idea what you're talking about. I simply—"

The woman in the large SUV in front of them flung her door open, bolted from the car, hopped twice to keep from being knocked down by the door, then dove into the dirt. The car kept rolling backwards.

"What in the —watch out!" Tallulah hollered.

Thump. The Lexus rolled into Eugenia's sedan.

The airbags deployed with a loud *pop.* Both women yelped in surprise.

"Oh, that smell is horrible," said Tallulah.

"Don't breathe that in. Whatever it is, it probably causes cancer or something just as bad."

"Well, what am I supposed to do? I have to breathe."

Vernon Markley appeared from somewhere, climbed into the Lexus, and then came out with the keys. "What happened? Are you all right?" He tried to hand the keys to the young woman who'd exited the car so dramatically, but she appeared to be having some sort of breakdown. Eyes wide open in horror, she just sat there unresponsive in the dirt. Then someone flipped her switch and she jumped up and rushed to the side of Eugenia's car.

"Oh, I am so, so sorry! Are y'all all right? Please tell me y'all are all right? Ma'am?"

Eugenia rolled down her window. She and Tallulah leaned over and smiled. "We're fine, darlin. Just a scratch, I'm sure. I'm surprised the airbags deployed at all. I imagine the size of your car was a factor."

"It's ridiculous, I know. I'm afraid I freaked out a little bit. There was a wasp inside my car. He flew straight at me."

"He didn't get you, did he?" Tallulah asked.

The young woman froze, seemed to take an inventory of all her systems. Then she smiled the loveliest smile. "No, thank goodness."

"Thank goodness, indeed," said Eugenia.

"I'm Quinn Poinsett, by the way," she said.

Eugenia and Tallulah introduced themselves.

"I'll just get my insurance information." Quinn stepped towards the passenger side of the Lexus.

A small crowd gathered. A familiar-looking blonde woman

who might've been forty or so and three tow-headed stair-step children climbed out of a golf cart and hurried over, stopping just a few feet away.

"That poor girl," said Eugenia. "Something's the matter with her."

"You mean the girl who hit us? Pretty thing, isn't she?" mused Tallulah. "What do you mean 'Something's the matter with her?'"

"Just look at her...she's a bundle of nerves. All jumpy. I wonder why."

"Hmm...well, looks like Birdie isn't home anyway."

Birdie Markley rushed over to the car. "Eugenia. Tallulah. Are y'all all right?"

"Birdie, it's good to see you. I was just telling Tallulah I wanted to come by for a visit. Do you know that young woman?"

"Yes—you know Redmond Poinsett?"

"Yes, of course. Nice young doctor," said Eugenia.

"I'd say he was in his early forties," said Tallulah.

"That's his wife," said Birdie.

"Is it really?" asked Eugenia, as if this were the most fascinating thing she'd heard lately.

"What's that face for?" asked Tallulah.

"It's a small island," said Eugenia. "I'm just surprised I've never met her, that's all. She's a good bit younger than he is, isn't she? I should know her, shouldn't I?" She unbuckled her seatbelt, opened the door and stepped out of the car.

"What are you up to now?" Tallulah muttered to the empty car seat. She shook her head and got out of the car. "Eugenia, we can't just leave the car sitting in the middle of the lot like this."

Quinn walked back around the front of her SUV and met Eugenia and Vernon at the spot where the two cars intersected. "I'm with State Farm. Should we call the police?" Quinn waved an insurance card.

Eugenia ran a hand over the hood of her car. "Let's not trouble them this afternoon. I don't think there's enough damage here to worry with all that."

"It's hard to tell," said Vernon. "Why don't you pull back into your parking spaces so we can get a better look at both cars?"

"Vernon, no one put you in charge here," Birdie said.

"I'm just trying to help."

"That's a fine idea, Vernon," said Tallulah. "Let's get out of folk's way."

"I guess we'd better go on inside," said Birdie. "We have a reservation."

"Are y'all going to be all right with this?" asked Vernon.

Eugenia gave him a look that was part eye roll, part wince. "I'm sure we can manage. Y'all go on ahead and enjoy your lunch."

"Text if you need me," said Vernon.

Birdie made a clucking noise and pulled her husband towards the restaurant.

"All right then." Eugenia smiled and waved. "Toodle-oo." When Vernon and Birdie were nearly up the steps Eugenia shook her head and said, "Why do men always think they're needed to manage things? Where were we?"

"Do you think it's okay to move the cars without having the police give us an okay on that?" Quinn bit her lip.

Eugenia dismissed the question with a wave. "The police have far more important things to worry about. Here, let's move out of the way." She climbed back into her car and pulled back into the spot she'd just vacated. Quinn followed suit, though she didn't look at all convinced that was the right idea.

The three of them scrutinized the back of the Lexus, which didn't have a mark on it, and the front end of Eugenia's Mercedes.

"It's just a scratch," said Eugenia. "I'm not worried about it in the least."

"Oh no, really—I'm happy to pay for that to be fixed," said Quinn. "And whatever needs to be done to the airbags, of course."

"Nonsense," said Eugenia. "I'm certain the detailer can buff that right out. It's nothing. But I tell you what, if you absolutely insist, why don't we exchange phone numbers? Then on the outside chance I'm wrong, I can give you a call. How would that be?"

Tallulah gave Eugenia a look that meant, *I know you're up to something here, and it has nothing to do with your car.*

"That's more than fair," said Quinn. "I insist you let me pay for any damage."

"Eugenia generally prefers to do all the insisting herself," said Tallulah.

Confusion flashed across Quinn's face, but she pulled a pad out of the shoulder bag she must've retrieved with the insurance information, scribbled down her phone number on a slip of paper, and handed it to Eugenia.

"Quinn? What's going on?" A woman of approximately Tallulah and Eugenia's generation strolled across the parking lot. She wore an elegant pantsuit, large sunglasses, and a brightly patterned scarf draped around her head and neck.

"Mamma," Quinn said. "Nothing to worry about. I accidentally backed into this lady's car, but there's no damage, so it's all good. Shall we go inside?" She offered Eugenia and Tallulah a wide smile and waved over her shoulder. "I'll look forward to hearing from you."

"If she only knew," murmured Tallulah.

"What are you carrying on about?"

"You are up to something. Are you planning to make that sweet young woman one of your projects?" asked Tallulah.

"Not at all," said Eugenia. "I'm going to make her yours."

"Exactly what do you mean by that?"

"I've remembered something you enjoy doing, but rarely did, because Henry was not a fan."

"No."

What do you mean, 'no?'"

"It was quite clear," said Tallulah.

"Tallulah, you love to entertain. I'd say Quinn needs a friend, wouldn't you?"

"She needs friends her own age, for Heaven's sake. I'm certain she has some."

"I'm not certain of that at all," said Eugenia. "What say let's bet on it?"

"Bet on it?"

"Yes. You'll ask Quinn and her husband, the handsome young doctor, to dinner. If Quinn has plenty of friends, and no time for new ones, she'll make an excuse. If she says no, I'll drop the whole thing."

Tallulah scoffed. "Humpf. Do I have your word on that?"

"Yes, of course. But you have to make it a sincere invitation."

"I can be sincere."

"Of course you can. I never suggested otherwise. Now, you'll need an escort."

"Eugenia—"

"How about Fish? No—Fish will be *my* escort. We'll figure out someone for you."

"What about Everette?"

"What about him? He'll still be off on his fishing tour, no doubt. Anyway, things are tense between us at the moment."

Tallulah could well imagine. She'd tolerated Everette for decades for Eugenia's sake, but since Eugenia was first diagnosed with cancer he'd proven himself a perfect horse's hind end. He'd abandoned her when she needed him most. It was inexcusable. He should be taken out and horsewhipped. Eugenia deserved so much better. "Fish will enjoy it I'm sure."

"Oh! I'm so happy you're getting into the spirit of things. Who else should we invite?" asked Eugenia.

"Don't push your luck."

Tallulah Meets Libba

Chapter Four

The following Thursday, April 13, 2017
Publix on Ben Sawyer Blvd
Mount Pleasant, South Carolina
Tallulah Wentworth

"How long will it be, do you suppose, before you let me go to the grocery store unattended?" Tallulah pulled a jar of pasta sauce from the shelf and perused the ingredients.

"Don't be absurd," said Eugenia. "I'm not here to *attend* you. It's the other way around. I still get so tired doing the simplest things. I'm not comfortable yet driving anywhere by myself."

Tallulah scrutinized her friend, sighed, and put the jarred sauce back on the shelf. The problem was, she couldn't be certain Eugenia didn't really need her. Chemotherapy was brutal, she knew that was true—that it took most people a long time to fully recover. But most of the time Eugenia seemed almost her old self, aside from the fact she was far too skinny.

"So you say." Tallulah gave Eugenia a level look, one that said, I see what you're trying to do no matter what you say. "How about I make us a pan of lasagne this evening?" Surely that would tempt her appetite. Just the thought of a deep dish of gooey, cheesy, meaty, messy lasagne made Tallulah's mouth water.

Eugenia perked up, her eyes wide and lit with enthusiasm. "That sounds wonderful. I have a recipe for a really good lentil lasagne."

Tallulah closed her eyes and lowered her head. Of course. It would have to be a *vegan* lasagna. "Why must you take all the joy out of eating? It's not healthy. And the reason you can't gain an ounce is because all you eat is leaves and twigs. You have got to eat something with some substance."

"I tell you what," said Eugenia. "You make this recipe for us, and if you don't like it enough to have seconds, tomorrow night we'll have whatever you like."

"Now that's a deal," said Tallulah. "What do we need from the store?"

"Some San Marzano tomatoes, whole wheat lasagne, and vegan cheese. I think I have everything else."

"Vegan cheese? Sounds like an abomination. What the devil do they make that out of?"

Eugenia put the lasagne noodles in the cart. "Some of it *is* an abomination. You have to be careful to buy the kind made from nuts, not oils."

"What sort of wine should we have with this mess?" asked Tallulah. "We'll need a lot of it."

"Whatever you want is fine with me. These tomatoes are on special. Let's get a dozen cans."

Tallulah stepped to the other side of the aisle and picked up one of the large cans. She pulled it closer to her face, then back trying to adjust her focus. "Here, now...these are not authentic San Marzano. That's probably why they're on sale."

"What do you mean they're not authentic San Marzanos? It says so right there on the label. 'Product of Italy.'"

"Not all Italian tomatoes are San Marzano."

"I am well aware of that, Tallulah. Look right there." Eugenia pointed to the words "San Marzano." "You need glasses."

"There's not a thing wrong with my eyesight," said Tallulah. "Where is the D.O.P. designation?"

"Oh, for goodness sake. It's right there." Eugenia pointed to the label. "This is the brand I buy all the time—well, when they're on special. They're ridiculous otherwise."

"I was reading just the other day how sometimes these labels are faked," said Tallulah.

"Well these are not fake. They're delicious," said Eugenia. "Now help me get twelve cans of them in the—" Eugenia turned around, her arms full, but their cart was gone.

"Where's the cart?" asked Tallulah.

"What did you do with it?" asked Eugenia.

"I haven't done anything with it. I've been standing here arguing with you about tomatoes. I think she took it."

They both looked down the aisle at the pert blonde woman in exercise gear, her ponytail swinging back and forth in time as she sped away, pushing a cart.

"Surely not," said Eugenia.

"Excuse me?" Tallulah hurried down the aisle after the blonde. "Excuse me?"

The woman didn't turn or show any indication of having heard Tallulah. She kept right on moving with purpose down the aisle.

Tallulah picked up her pace. Just as the woman reached the end of the aisle, Tallulah reached out and put a hand on her shoulder.

The woman stopped and turned, a question on her face.

Tallulah looked in the cart. It was theirs all right. "Pardon me, but I believe you may have taken our cart by mistake."

The woman popped her earbuds out. "I'm sorry?"

"I believe you took our cart by mistake." Tallulah tilted her head when she smiled, like she was saying, It's okay, we've all done it, when actually, Tallulah was fairly certain she never had. Young women were awfully distracted these days. They had so many gadgets to continuously monitor, cell phones, watches, earbuds...

who knew what all else? This particular young woman looked familiar. Did she know her?

The woman's face screwed up in confusion. She looked at the cart. "Oh. Oh my goodness! That's not my cart. I am so sorry."

"No worries." Tallulah reached for the cart handle just as the woman tried to turn it around. "Excuse me."

They both laughed.

Eugenia, who'd meandered down the aisle, joined them. "Hello," she said. "I think we may have seen you at The Obstinate Daughter on Sunday afternoon."

"Yes, of course," said Tallulah. "That's where I know you from. Do you live on Sullivan's Island?"

"I do," said the young woman. "I'm Libba Graham."

"I'm Eugenia Ladson, and the woman who accosted you is my dear friend Tallulah Wentworth."

"Oh, she didn't accost me at all," said Libba. "I'm so sorry I took your cart. How embarrassing. I'm afraid my mind was elsewhere. Trying to get everything done before I pick up the kids at school."

Tallulah smiled and nodded wistfully. It was very likely exhausting being a mother in the age of helicopter parenting, but Tallulah would give anything to switch places with her and experience the everyday joy of grocery shopping for her children, then picking them up from school.

"Please don't give it a second thought," said Eugenia. "How long have you lived on Sullivan's Island?"

"My husband, Jake and I moved here from Nashville. It'll be a year ago in July," said Libba.

"Well, it was nice—" Tallulah started to pull the cart away and bumped into Eugenia, who apparently had no intentions of concluding their conversation.

"It's a gorgeous place to live," said Eugenia. "I live in Charleston myself, on Tradd, though at the moment I'm staying with Tallulah indefinitely. She's lived on Sullivan's Island her entire life, so, ages, actually." She grinned slyly at Tallulah.

Tallulah raised an eyebrow. "The length of your stay is getting shorter by the moment."

"I'm thinking of buying a house on Sullivan's Island myself," said Eugenia. "We'll see how things go. Perhaps..." Her smile faltered.

"Well, we love it," said Libba. "It was—"

"I bet you've barely had a chance to meet anyone, as busy as you are." Eugenia aborted Libba's attempt at extricating herself from the conversation. "Tallulah and I are having a dinner party next month, on May 27. We'd love for you and your husband to come. It would give you an opportunity to meet a few of your neighbors you perhaps haven't yet."

Libba opened her mouth, hesitated, then said, "Thank you so much for the invitation. I'll check with Jake."

"I do realize that's the Saturday of Memorial Day weekend," said Eugenia. "I hope that won't prove to be a problem."

"Maybe we should exchange phone numbers?" suggested Libba.

Eugenia handed Libba her phone. "An excellent idea. If you don't mind, just send yourself a text from my phone. Then we'll be connected. Tallulah and I will reach out with more details soon."

Libba did as she was asked. Everyone always did with Eugenia. There was something about her that just made it nearly impossible for people to refuse her. Tallulah knew this better than most.

"It was lovely meeting y'all." Libba handed Eugenia's phone back with a smile. "I guess I'd better find my own grocery cart. Bye."

"Bye now," called Eugenia as Libba dashed off down the aisle, retracing her steps.

"What exactly are you up to?" asked Tallulah. "We had a deal, you and I. If Quinn turned down my invitation—"

"Well, I figured it would be nice for Quinn to have someone closer to her own age at dinner. That way it's not odd, her being in a group of geriatrics. I wonder if they know each other," mused

Eugenia. "We can ask Camille Houston if you like. She'll bring a date. And of course Birdie and Vernon. That'll give us ten. That should be enough for a dinner party, don't you think?"

"What I think is that you can't count. That would make twelve of us," said Tallulah.

Eugenia's forehead creased as she tilted her head in thought. "Yes, of course. You're entirely correct. Good. Twelve is definitely a good number for a dinner party."

"You're really going to make me go through with this, aren't you?" asked Tallulah.

"Naturally. So you haven't called Quinn yet?"

"I haven't gotten around to it."

"Well, I suppose you'd better call this afternoon. It's a little over six weeks away. We don't want to wait until the last minute. That would be rude."

"I hadn't realized we'd set a date," said Tallulah, "for the dinner party at my house, that wasn't even definite yet until you invited Libba and her husband just now."

"Hmm." Eugenia raised her eyebrows. "I'm sure we discussed it. What do you think we should serve? We need a theme…"

"A theme? It's dinner. Dinner is the theme."

"If I didn't know better, I'd suspect you'd never been to a proper dinner party. Now…let's find that vegan cheese."

"I'd rather hunt a rattlesnake."

"And then we need to locate your sunny disposition," said Eugenia.

"What I need to locate is a big enough bottle of Valium to put me out of my misery."

"I'm going to need to get some more clothes from the house," said Eugenia. "The weather is warming up, and I can't imagine leaving you on your own recognizance in the foreseeable future."

Frances & Tallulah Meet Sarabeth

Chapter Five

Tuesday, *March 16, 2021 7:05 a.m.*
Sullivan's Island, South Carolina
Boone Home, I'On Avenue
Sarabeth Mercer Jackson Boone

I was in the kitchen, up to my eyeballs in boxes, when the doorbell rang for the first time that Tuesday morning. The moving trucks had unloaded the Saturday before, and we were still living in utter chaos, but giddy. Our dream had finally come true. Tucker and I were residents of Sullivan's Island. This was before the house started falling down around our ears.

There was something sticky on my hand. Absently, I grabbed a paper towel and dashed for the door. There wasn't a peep hole, a fact I was just then noticing. When I swung the door open, a small, white-haired lady waited on my front porch holding a cake carrier.

"Hey there," I said enthusiastically. I offered her my sunniest smile as I wiped my hands.

"Hello," she said. "I'm Frances Tennant. I live a couple blocks over, on Atlantic. Welcome to the neighborhood! I've brought you a pound cake." She spoke with a delightful British accent, and wore a genuine smile. Her pixie haircut gave her an impish look.

"Oh! How sweet of you! Thank you so much. Please forgive my appearance but we're just unpacking."

"I quite understand," she said. "No worries a'tall. I hope you're not gluten intolerant. I'm afraid I didn't think of that. So many people are these days."

"No, not at all," I said. "And I simply adore pound cake."

"Oh, good." She handled me the cake carrier. "Well, it was nice meeting you. If you need anything a'tall as you're getting settled, please don't hesitate to call. My number's taped to the bottom of the cake plate."

We said our goodbyes and I closed the door. Frances Tennant was the first neighbor I'd met, and she was just precious. I was smiling as I went back to my stack of boxes.

Thirty minutes later, I was making myself a glass of iced tea to go with the best pound cake I'd had in recent memory, when the doorbell rang for the second time that morning. I pulled the door open to see another woman I didn't know wearing the sort of athleisure outfit some ladies wore for exercise.

"I'm terribly sorry to bother you," she said, "but I was out walking just now, and I'm afraid I'm not feeling well. Could I trouble you for a glass of water?"

"Yes, of course, please come in." Was she having a medical emergency? Should I call 9-1-1? I stepped back to let her in and closed the door behind her. "Please have a seat in the family room." I gestured vaguely towards the sofa. Moving quickly, I crossed through the breakfast area and into the kitchen. The house had an open floor plan, with the main living area—family room, dining room, breakfast area and kitchen—all one big room, really, separated only by small sections of wall framing over-sized pass-thru doorways.

"I'm Tallulah Wentworth," she said as she took a seat on the sofa.

"Nice to meet you," I said. "I'm Sarabeth Boone." I hurried back with a glass of water.

"Oh, thank you so much." She sipped the water and closed her eyes for a moment. "I don't know what's come over me. I'm still a bit dizzy, I'm afraid. Is it all right if I sit here for a few moments?"

"Why, of course. You just sit right here until you feel better. Do you live nearby?" I asked.

"Yes, just a few blocks east, on the other side of the elementary school and the library. I'm on Atlantic Avenue, between Stations 21 and 22. Parts of Atlantic Avenue are front row, but Pettigrew runs between that section of Atlantic and the beach."

"I know exactly where you're talking about," I said. "I'd be happy to run you home if you'd like." She shouldn't be walking home. Something serious could be wrong.

"Oh, that's not necessary. I'm certain I'll be fine in a moment. You've just moved in, haven't you?"

"Yes—my husband, Tucker, and I moved in three days ago. We're not really settled yet. We have a lot of updates planned. It's been a while since this house has had any TLC."

"I'm afraid Paul Johnson was in ill health for quite some time," said Tallulah. "He just wasn't able to keep up with things, and Irene was busy taking care of him."

"That's what we heard," I said. "It sounded like a sad situation."

"It was indeed," said Tallulah. "I know they were grateful to find buyers who seemed to love the house."

"Aww—we really do. It's a dream come true for us."

Tallulah's gaze seemed to have landed on a crack in the wall over the pass-through to the breakfast room. It hadn't been there when we'd done the walk through before closing. "I'm sure there's a lot to be done."

"More things are being added to the list all the time." At that time, I had no idea whatsoever what was in store. I was blissfully ignorant of a great many things.

Tallulah finished the glass of water and set the empty glass on a coaster. "I so appreciate your hospitality. Please allow me to return the favor."

"Oh, that's not necessary at all. You're more than welcome."

"Please, I insist," said Tallulah. "I have a little group that comes to my house once a month for supper club. It started about four years ago with just a random Saturday night dinner, and now it's something we all look forward to every month. We'd love for you and your husband to join us. It'll give y'all an opportunity to meet some more of your neighbors."

"Supper club?" I grinned like a fool. I had wanted to be in a supper club forever. The idea of it just conjured visions of adults enjoying an elegant meal and interesting conversation. "That sounds just lovely—thank you so much for the kind invitation. What can we bring?"

"Not a thing." She waved the notion away. "Planning supper club keeps me occupied and out of trouble. We have a different theme every month. I think this time it's going to be Italian, perhaps, 'A Taste of La Dolce Vita.' I'm in the mood for pasta. Maybe we'll stomp on some grapes and make wine."

"Well..." I smiled like perhaps that last part was a joke, hoping that it was. "... if you're sure. Please let me know if you change your mind. Now, when is it?"

"It's always the last Saturday of the month, and it's always at my house, unless I decide to change it, but I never have yet." Tallulah rose. "I'm feeling much better now. Thank you again. I do appreciate your kindness."

"My pleasure."

"Here's my phone number and my address." Tallulah handed me a heavy cream-colored card. "When you have a moment, text me your phone number just in case. At my age any number of things could come up, couldn't they?"

After we' said our goodbyes and I closed the door behind her, I stared at her elegant card and dreamed just a couple beats of a happy dream involving a long outdoor table with lights strung overhead. Then I got back to unpacking boxes. I had no idea just then how many ways Tallulah Wentworth would change my life.

Sarabeth Gets to Know Frances Tennant

Chapter Six

Friday, March 19, 2021 3:30 p.m.
Home of Mrs. Frances Tennant
Sarabeth Mercer Jackson Boone

"Goodness, what a mess," said Frances.

She'd asked how things were going with our move-in, and I'd told her all about the air conditioning going out. I'd thought I would just drop the cake plate at the door, but Frances seemed quite eager for me to come in for a visit. I didn't have the heart to turn her down. She was a widow, I'd learned, and lived by herself. We were having tea and carrot cake in her living room.

"It's not such a big deal right now. It's just March," I said. "But I've got to find someone to fix it before it gets hot. I've never dealt with anything quite like it. I'm telling you, all the tradesmen are booked out months in advance. It's hard to find people available to do anything right now. I've heard it's something to do with the aftermath of Covid."

"Not the most advantageous time to have a fixer-upper on your hands, I imagine," said Frances. "And who would have known it would be so hard to find available tradesmen? I tell you what...try George Riley. His company's called Cool Breeze Air. He's reasonable and reliable."

"Thank you so much. I will surely give him a call."

"Tell him I sent you, and that he should get to you right away. I'm a retired English teacher. George was one of my students." She smiled mischievously. "He'll get it sorted. If it gets warmer and you need a cool place to sleep in the meantime, you and your husband are welcome to stay here."

"Oh, I'm sure that won't be necessary—but thank you so much."

"Such a hassle to have this happen while you're moving in. But what doesn't kill you makes you stronger, right? That's what they say, anyhow." A troubled look crossed her face.

"Is everything all right?"

"Oh, yes. Everything's fine. Would you like more tea? More cake?"

"No, thank you. This carrot cake is every bit as delicious as your pound cake. Do you bake often?"

"I keep a cake in the house. It's nice to have something if someone stops by. And I do enjoy a slice."

"I admit I'm a little envious that you can eat cake regularly and stay so slim," I said.

"At my age I don't worry so much about my weight anymore." Her phone dinged. She glanced at the screen. A pained look flashed across her face. "What is the matter with people?"

I waited for her to explain.

After a moment, she said, "Sometimes I think Facebook and the like—social media—will be the downfall of civilization."

"I don't spend much time on all that myself. I mean, well, I'm an author, so I'm there to chat with readers, on my professional page. But I don't stay in touch with friends and family there."

"I'm afraid it's where I get most of the updates on my family. We're so spread out. I still have family in England, and my children and grandchildren are all in California," said Frances. "An author, you say? Isn't that something? What sort of books do you write?"

"Mystery novels—nothing too violent. They're on the cozy side."

"How lovely. Well, I'll have to check you out. Do they have your books in the library?"

I smiled and nodded. "As a matter of fact, they do."

Her phone dinged again. She picked it up, swiped, and tapped. "Forgive me. I'm afraid I'm letting these people get to me."

I squinted at her. "Is someone harassing you online?" Who would be unkind to this sweet, diminutive grandmother? I immediately felt protective of her. Oh my stars! *I* was a grandmother. Sometimes I forgot that little detail. No wonder all the checkout girls called me sweetie and dear anymore. They looked at me like I looked at Frances, with an eye towards looking out for me, since I was clearly in my dotage. I surely didn't *feel* like a grandmother. Inside I felt exactly the same as I did the day I married Tucker. I was twenty-six years old. Did Frances still feel twenty-six too? My guess was she was somewhere in the vicinity of Mamma's age.

"Yes, they are, actually." She sighed wearily. "I'm afraid I brought it on myself."

What on earth? I tilted my head and leaned in towards her with a look that said, I have a very sympathetic ear.

"Well, I opened my mouth, didn't I?" She scoffed at herself. "You'll soon find that the most controversial topic in our little town is not politics."

"Religion?"

"Trees," she said with raised eyebrows over the top of her teacup.

"*Trees?*" I felt my squint deepen and I might've blinked at her a few times.

"Surely someone told you about the trees."

"No, they didn't. What's wrong with the trees?" Was there some kind of fungus that threatened all the trees on the island?

Were we losing our shade canopy? Our yard had one anyway. And the lovely palmetto palms...

"Nothing is wrong with them. Surely you've read about all this in the newspaper. There've been lawsuits..."

I shook my head. "I don't have the first clue what you're talking about. I watch about five minutes of the news, occasionally. There's so rarely any good news anymore. I figure if there's something I need to know, Tucker will tell me."

"Oh, dear. Where to start? You know how most sea islands are constantly fighting erosion? They bring sand in periodically to renourish the beaches because they're forever washing away."

"Yes, of course."

"Sullivan's Island has that problem on the northeastern end, but the rest of the island is actually growing because sediment that would otherwise be washed on down to Folly Beach or other points south is accreting to Sullivan's Island. It's the opposite of erosion. This has been going on since the jetties went in. They started those in 1878, mind you, to fix the problems with Charleston Harbor."

I had only the vaguest idea what jetties were, why we actually built them in the first place, but that was okay, because Frances was in the mood to tell me all about them.

"They're two massive underwater walls of rocks, laid out rather like a funnel, with the small end towards the ocean. Before the jetties, Charleston Harbor had three separate channels, each approaching at a different angle—none very deep. At low water, the best approach was only about nine feet deep. There were sandbars...it was difficult to navigate.

"So they built these three-mile-long underwater stone walls. One of them juts out from Sullivan's Island, the other from Morris Island. They created one deep channel that comes directly into the harbor. It took seventeen years and more than a million tons of stone. And I suppose it does what they designed it to do quite nicely.

"The trouble is, the resulting changes in the way sediment

behaves wiped out Morris Island nearly completely, and damaged Folly Beach. And Sullivan's Island gets the windfall, if you will. Even before the channel was built, all the way back in the 1840s, they built Bowman's Jetty, to help with erosion around Fort Moultrie. And that did help, from what I understand. But once the harbor jetties went in, well, everything changed."

I might've been giving her a confused look.

"I do go on a bit, don't I?" asked Frances. "Yes...the trees. Over time, as sediment builds, you get new dunes on the beach. Then come grasses, flowers, then shrubs. Along the way, you may get another row of dunes or two. Eventually, trees begin to grow and a forest is born. Today, we have a maritime forest of nearly two hundred acres that technically reaches almost to Breach Inlet. It's nothing but sea oats, flowers, and a shrub or two on the northeast end. But it's a thriving stand of a hundred and twenty-five or more different kinds of plants and trees—wax myrtles, cedars, pines, magnolias, and young live oaks and on and on, on our end of the island."

"I bet it's just lovely," I said, feeling stupid for not knowing any of this.

"It really is. And the birds...so many different kinds of birds. So...the newly accreted land belongs to the town, not to the individuals who bought the lots closest to the ocean. As it happens, back in 1991, the town realized our great bounty could give rise to problems. They sold the land for $10 to the Lowcountry Open Land Trust. That's a nonprofit corporation created to preserve natural areas. The land trust in turn, deeded the property back to the town, but with deed restrictions. Essentially, the land must be left in its natural state, but the town has the authority to take measures to control the vegetation as deemed necessary for the common good. There's a provision in there somewhere that the agreement can be modified, but it requires a unanimous council vote and approval of seventy-five percent of voters in a referendum, so that's highly unlikely."

"I'm still struggling—"

"Come look out my windows." She pulled me over to get a good look. Her house appeared to be standing on a grassy oasis dotted with palm trees in the middle of a forest.

"When Richard and I built this house in 1975, it was ocean front. We had fabulous views and the most wonderful ocean breeze. It was spectacular."

"That's incredible. You would never know the Atlantic Ocean is right on the other side of—"

"Yes. All those trees and shrubs. Quite. They weren't there in 1975, and little in the way of vegetation was there on September 21, 1989."

I gasped. "Hugo." Now there was something I knew about.

"Yes. Hurricane Hugo nearly demolished our home. It did demolish the homes of many of our friends. This entire island disappeared under the sea for nearly an hour. And afterwards...it was like living through the aftermath of an atomic bomb. Hugo left us with a bridge sideways up, boats on land, houses in the middle of the street, fish in houses, no utilities, and snakes everywhere."

"I can't even imagine."

"No one can, unless they've lived through it. And that's precisely why some of my neighbors desperately want to cut the trees so they can see the ocean and feel the breezes. They can't imagine. Or they're complacent because it hasn't happened in thirty-odd years. But that's how long it had been when Hugo hit."

"And who is harassing you online?" I was still squinting a bit.

"I'm a bit of an activist." She grinned. "I volunteer with the Coastal Conservation League and donate generously to their causes. I'm also a member of Sullivan's Island for All, a group of local residents committed to protecting the maritime forest. I offer my opinions freely. My mistake was joining a community group online. It's not official—nothing organized by the town. It's just a bunch of people who live here."

"Your *neighbors* are harassing you?" I asked in disbelief.

"*Our* neighbors, yes."

"That's outrageous."

"You wouldn't believe what people will say when they don't have to say it to your face. One of them told me I needed to be forcibly moved to an old folks home."

"What? I just cannot believe that. Who said such a thing to you?"

She waved a hand. "It's not important. I don't know the man. He hasn't lived here but a couple years. He was fast friends with some of the folks in favor of cutting everything back. And he has an unfortunate tendency to sound off online. I suspect he's an insomniac who has a drink or two in the middle of the night and gets on Facebook. He's annoying, but harmless. Join the group—it's for people who live here. And it comes in handy if there's a power outage, or the bridge gets backed up, or someone's dog goes missing. That's why I joined. It's a handy way to reach many of your neighbors quickly to get word out when you need to."

"They shouldn't allow folks to be obnoxious in there," I said.

"Well, someone has to moderate it, but no one wants to police their neighbors."

"I suppose I can see that."

"Anyway, I'm sorry to disappoint him—the 'gentleman' in question—but Richard and I built this house, and all but rebuilt it after Hugo. I've lived here forty-six years. And I'm not moving anywhere."

"You know, I think I will join that group. It is a good idea to be able to get in touch with people, especially with me not knowing anyone. We're so new. There aren't many people I could call." Perhaps I could put this cretin in his place next time he attacked Frances.

"Yes, of course you should join. The foolishness is aggravating sometimes, but it can also be entertaining."

"And I'm going to look into Sullivan's Island for All and the Coastal Conservation League."

"Oh, that would be lovely," said Frances.

"Tucker and I plan to make this our permanent home," I said. "We need to get involved in things."

"We certainly need everyone we can get," said Frances. "It's an ongoing battle. It will never be settled any longer than it takes someone new to come up with a new angle of attack."

"Where does it stand now?"

"Well, they've been arguing about it for decades, going back and forth. Every time a compromise was reached, the cutters wanted to cut more. It was never enough. Then a couple of my neighbors filed a lawsuit in 2010. They basically wanted unlimited cutting. It went all the way to the State Supreme Court. Then the town reached a mediated compromise with the plaintiffs that involved far more cutting than should ever be allowed. That was in October of last year.

"There was a bit of a hoodwink, you see. Two new council members were elected who were, shall we say, less than forthcoming about where they stood on the issue. Honestly, I'm not sure everyone understood the election was primarily about the maritime forest. The settlement was approved on the slimmest of margins, and allowed for massive cutting. But hopefully that won't be the end of it. There's a new election coming up May 4. Make sure you're registered to vote."

"Oh, I definitely will do that very thing."

"Just don't make the mistake I did and attempt a rational discussion on the issue in the Facebook group. I'm old enough I should know better. But not in need of an old folks home, thank you very much."

Recipes...

Eugenia's Chicken Bog

Ingredients:

1 (4 to 5 pound) whole chicken *
6 – 8 cups liquid, more or less depending on the bird, the pot, and
the phase of the moon **
2 pounds smoked beef sausage ***
¼ cup unsalted butter (½ stick), divided by tablespoons
4 tablespoons olive oil
½ – 1 teaspoon red pepper flakes to taste (this might vary
depending on your sausage choice)
3 cups long grain white rice, rinsed ****
9 cups reserved broth (from step one below or cartons from the
grocery store if the purists don't bother you and you're short on
time)
1 large piece Parmesan cheese rind
2 – 3 ounces fresh grated Parmesan cheese
1 tablespoon lemon juice
Chopped parsley or scallions

* If you prefer, you could use 3 pounds of chicken breasts, but the
purists will bless your heart. You can even skip straight to step two

below by using Costco rotisserie chicken if you want to, but Eugenia worries about the sodium and the phosphorous in store-bought cooked chicken.

** Historically, water is what was used. The results will be richer if you add some chicken broth or bone broth into the mix. The ratio is up to you, but if you're using only chicken breasts, you'll want to consider the bone broth. We'll get precise with the liquid measurement later in the recipe.

*** You can use Kielbasa or Andouille or any other sausage you like.

**** If you prefer to use a different type of rice, just be sure to adjust the liquid amount and cooking time if necessary. Also, the purists...

What you give the chicken (or, Aromatics / Seasonings for the broth)
3 stalks celery, roughly chopped
1 large yellow onion, roughly chopped
6 cloves garlic, roughly chopped
2 ½ teaspoon salt (not iodized)
2 teaspoon ground black pepper (fresh ground is best)
1 ½ teaspoon paprika
½ teaspoon dried thyme
1 bay leaf

Note: If you're using mostly pre-made broth for your liquid, you could cut back on some of these if you like. Eugenia believes making a good broth is an art and we should all express ourselves.

What you give the rice (or, vegetables, seasonings, et cetera for the rice)
2 stalks celery, minced

3 cloves garlic, minced, more if you like
1 ½ cups carrots, chopped small (Eugenia adds these. A lot of folks don't. The purists likely bless Eugenia's heart, but she is undaunted.)
2 leeks, finely chopped, about ½ c. (This is Eugenia's secret ingredient. See note above on the purists.)
½ cup minced onion

Directions:

1. Cook the chicken and make the broth.
2. Discard anything unsightly that came inside the chicken.
3. Put the chicken in a large pot.
4. Add broth / water mixture, roughly chopped celery, onion, and garlic, salt, pepper, paprika, thyme, and bay leaf.
5. Make sure you have enough liquid to just cover the chicken.
6. Cover the pot and bring to a simmer. Once it's bubbly, reduce the heat to low and cook until the chicken is very tender. The legs and thighs should pull apart easily at this point. Be careful not to boil. That will make the chicken tough and dry, and nobody likes tough dry chicken. For a whole chicken, this step should take 2 ½ -3 hours. If you're using the breast only, it should be about 25 minutes. Check one of the larger pieces to make sure it's as done as you like it.
7. While the chicken is cooking, prep the remaining vegetables.
8. Remove the chicken from the pot and set aside to cool.
9. Strain the broth through a fine mesh strainer, discarding all the vegetables, skin, bones, et cetera.

10. Taste the broth now, before it cools, and determine if you're going to want more salt and / or black pepper.
11. When the chicken is cool enough, shred it. Discard skin, bones, anything unsightly.
12. Mince the celery, garlic, and onion.
13. Chop the carrots.
14. Rinse the leeks, then cut off the bottom root end. Remove the tough, darker green portion of the leaves, leaving only the pale green and white portion. Quarter these. Wash thoroughly, separating all the layers. Leeks are notorious for trapping dirt and sand between their layers.
15. Thinly slice the leek quarters.
16. Cut the sausage into bite-sized pieces.
17. Melt a tablespoon of the butter in a 12-inch cast iron skillet.
18. Brown the sausage in the skillet, about 7 – 10 minutes, adding the red pepper flakes a minute or two in.
19. Deglaze the pan with one cup of the reserved broth.
20. Remove the pan from the heat.
21. Add 3 tablespoons butter to a large pot or Dutch oven.
22. Add prepared celery, carrots, onion, and leeks.
23. Cook until vegetables start to brown, about 7- 9 minutes.
24. Add garlic and cook and stir about a minute.
25. Add olive oil and stir.
26. Add the rice, toasting in the pot until coated and golden, about 4 minutes. Add additional olive oil or butter if necessary to coat the rice.
27. Add remaining reserved broth and deglaze.
28. Add the sausage to the Dutch oven, scraping the pan well.

29. Add additional salt and black pepper if needed, to taste.
30. Add the Parmesan rind to the pot.
31. Bring to a boil then cover. Reduce heat to low / medium-low to gently simmer.
32. Cook until rice is tender, 18 – 20 minutes. This may vary depending on the specific rice used.
33. Remove rind, stir in chicken.
34. Cover, remove from heat, and let rest for 10 minutes.
35. As you serve, sprinkle with lemon juice, top with parmesan cheese and scallions.

Gavin's Air Fried Green Tomatoes

~~∞~~

Ingredients:

3 green tomatoes, sliced ¼-inch thick
1 teaspoon sea salt, divided
½ teaspoon black pepper
2 cups whole wheat flour
2 teaspoons garlic powder
1 cup cashew milk
1 cup whole-wheat panko breadcrumbs
1 cup cornmeal
Olive oil cooking spray

Directions:

1. Preheat convection oven / oven with air fryer to 425 degrees, or countertop air fryer to 400 degrees.
2. Pat tomato slices dry with paper towels.
3. Sprinkle with salt and pepper.
4. Stir flour, ½ teaspoon salt, and garlic powder together in a shallow dish.
5. Place cashew milk in a separate shallow dish.

6. Stir panko and cornmeal together in a third shallow dish.
7. Dredge the tomato slices in the flour mixture, then dip in cashew milk, then dredge in the panko mixture.
8. Place slices on a baking sheet or place a single layer in countertop air fryer.
9. Coat the tomatoes well with cooking spray.
10. Cook until crispy and golden on one side, about 4 minutes.
11. Flip the tomato slices; coat with cooking spray and cook until golden and crispy on reverse side, about 4 minutes.
12. Transfer to a plate. If using a countertop air fryer, repeat the procedure with the remaining tomatoes.
13. Enjoy these in any way you like, but Gavin recommends them on top of a salad with ranch dressing!

Gavin's House Macaroni & Cheese

~~~~

Ingredients:

1 pound pasta (Gavin uses Campanelle or Cavatelli, but elbows are fine)
1 tablespoon vegan butter (Gavin likes MiYokos European Style)
2 ¼ cups raw cashews
2 cups water
4 ½ tablespoons fresh lemon juice
¾ cup nutritional yeast
2 teaspoons garlic powder
⅜ teaspoon turmeric
½ teaspoon dry mustard
2 teaspoons salt
¼ teaspoon black pepper
10 ounces nut-based vegan cheddar cheese (Gavin likes Dare or Rebel)
4 ounces nut-based vegan cream cheese (Gavin only uses MiYokos)
4 tablespoons vegan butter
3 cups Panko bread crumbs (plain)
Halved cherry tomatoes

Scallions, chopped

Directions:

1. Preheat oven to 350 degrees.
2. Boil pasta according to package directions, drain, and return to pot. Set aside near stove with lid to keep warm.
3. Place cashews in heat-proof glass bowl or measuring cup.
4. Pour boiling water over cashews and soak ten minutes.
5. Drain soaking water and discard.
6. Place soaked, drained cashews in a Vitamix or similar high-powered blender.
7. Add 2 cups fresh water, lemon juice, nutritional yeast, garlic powder, turmeric, mustard, salt, pepper, and both vegan cheeses.
8. Blend until very smooth.
9. Taste and adjust seasonings or add more water to desired consistency and re-blend.
10. Pour sauce over pasta in pot and mix well.
11. Butter a large casserole dish with vegan butter. If you have a 4-quart dish (14 x 10) it should all fit.
12. Pour noodle and sauce mixture into prepared pan.
13. Make a topping of melted butter and Panko bread crumbs.
14. Sprinkle topping over casserole.
15. Place desired number of halved cherry tomatoes on top.
16. Bake 20 minutes or until bubbly and slightly browned on top.
17. Sprinkle on scallions during last five minutes.

Gavin's Olé Mole Enchiladas

Ingredients:

Enchiladas
12 large whole wheat or corn tortillas (corn are harder to work with)
1 batch Bean Filling (see below)
1 batch Cashew Cheez (see below)
1 batch Fajita Vegetables (see below)
1 batch Gavin's Olé Mole Sauce to taste
1 jar Vegan Valley Queso
1 can Hatch Green Enchilada sauce, warmed
Vegan Sour Cream
Fresh Pico de Gallo
Chopped cilantro
Chopped green onions

Bean Filling
2 cans black beans, drained
1 cup frozen fire roasted corn, thawed
1/2 cup vegan sour cream
1/2 cup picante

1/4 cup chopped cilantro
1 tablespoon lime juice
2 teaspoons canned chipotle pepper in adobo sauce (more or less to taste)
1-2 garlic cloves
1 teaspoon salt
1/2 teaspoon black pepper

Cashew Cheez
3 cups raw cashews
4 cups (approximately – doesn't have to be exact) boiling water
2 1/2 tablespoons lemon juice
1/2 teaspoon garlic powder
1/2 teaspoon salt
1/2 teaspoon fresh ground black pepper
1/2 – 3/4 cup water

Fajita Vegetables
2 tablespoons olive oil
2 large red peppers sliced
1 large red onion thinly sliced
1 medium zucchini sliced into half moons
1/2 teaspoon dried Mexican oregano
Salt to taste
Black pepper to taste

Olé Mole Sauce
2 tablespoons Oil
2 cups diced yellow onion
1/4 cup chili powder
1 teaspoon ancho chili powder
1/8 – 1/2 teaspoon Chipotle powder, depending on spice preference*
2 teaspoons Mexican oregano
1 teaspoon garlic powder

1/2 teaspoon ground cumin
1 teaspoon cinnamon
1/8 teaspoon cloves
2 ounces Mexican chocolate, chopped coarse
4 cloves garlic, minced
4 cups low sodium vegetable broth
3/4 cup tomato paste Muir Glen organic or Cento (one small can)
1/2 cup almond butter
1/4 cup maple syrup
1/4 cup raisins
2 tablespoons toasted sesame seeds
1 teaspoon salt
Additional salt and black pepper to taste

* 1/2 teaspoon of chipotle powder makes it pretty spicy—I wouldn't want it any spicier, personally. Some family members would like it better with less.

Directions:

Olé Mole Sauce

1. Gather ingredients.
2. Measure the spices into a small bowl.
3. Heat oil in a large saucepan over medium-high heat.
4. Add onion and sauté, stirring occasionally, until soft and translucent, 5-7 minutes.
5. Add chili powders, Mexican oregano, garlic powder, cumin, cinnamon, cloves, and Mexican chocolate. Cook and stir until everything is evenly mixed and chocolate is bubbly.
6. Add minced garlic and sauté for 1-2 more minutes, stirring occasionally.

7. Stir in broth, tomato paste, maple syrup, raisins, almond butter, sesame seeds, and the 1 teaspoon of salt and bring to simmer.
8. Reduce heat to medium and simmer gently, stirring occasionally, until slightly thickened, about 15 minutes.
9. Transfer to a blender, and process until very smooth, about 1 minute. Depending on the size of your blender, you may need to do this in batches.
10. Return fully blended sauce to pan and return to simmer.
11. Reduce heat to medium-low. Taste, and season the sauce with more salt, pepper, and maple syrup to taste.
12. Simmer until thickened to desired consistency.
13. Use immediately, or ideally, cool and refrigerate 24 hours in sealed container to let flavors marry.

Bean Filling

1. Mash beans with a pastry blender or potato masher.
2. Stir in all other bean filling ingredients until incorporated.
3. Set aside Bean Filling.

Cashew Cheez

1. Soak cashews in boiling water for an hour. Drain completely and discard water.
2. Pulse cashews, lemon juice, garlic powder, salt, and pepper in a high-speed blender until the nuts are chopped.
3. Blend and gradually add water until desired spreadable but thick consistency is reached.
4. Set aside Cheez.

Fajita Vegetables

1. Heat oil in a large cast iron skillet over medium-high heat until shimmering.
2. Add veggies.
3. Add salt, pepper, and oregano as veggies cook, stirring occasionally until crisp but tender, about 5-6 minutes.

Enchiladas

1. Make the mole sauce the day before and refrigerate.
2. Make the three fillings: Bean, Cashew Chez, and Fajita Veggies.
3. Preheat the oven to 400.
4. Warm the tortillas slightly to make them easier to work with.
5. Spray 2 13×9 casserole dishes lightly with olive oil.
6. Cover the bottom of the dishes with mole sauce.
7. To assemble the enchiladas: spread each tortilla with about 1/4 c. Cashew Cheez, 1/3 c. Bean Filling, and some Fajita Veggies.
8. Roll tightly and place, seam-side down in prepared dish. Note: We can only get six enchiladas in a dish without overcrowding.
9. Pour mole sauce over the top. Some folks like me like a lot of sauce. To others, less is better. It's up to you.
10. Bake 30 – 45 minutes or until the temperature in the middle reaches 160 degrees.
11. Remove from oven and let sit for 5 – 10 minutes.
12. Plate two enchiladas each and top with warmed queso, warmed Hatch enchilada sauce, and your choice of vegan sour cream, Pico de Gallo, green onions, and extra cilantro.

Hadley's Black Bean & Mango Salad

Ingredients:

Salad
2 15-ounce cans black beans, drained and rinsed
2 small mangos, diced
2 avocados, diced
1 cup corn kernels (fresh or frozen) *
1 red bell pepper, diced
½ of a red onion, chopped
½ cup chopped scallions
¼ cup fresh cilantro, chopped
1 small jalapeño, seeded and diced (optional)
Salt and pepper to taste (add after dressing) **

* Fresh corn on the cob is our favorite, but if that's not handy or you're in a time crunch, the fire roasted frozen corn works well in this recipe.

** I'm generous with the salt and pepper.

Dressing

½ cup fresh squeezed orange juice
¼ cup fresh squeezed lime juice
3 tablespoons agave nectar, more or less to taste
½ teaspoon chili powder

Directions:

1. Toss salad ingredients in a large bowl.
2. Mix dressing ingredients.
3. Pour dressing over salad and mix well.
4. Add salt and pepper to taste.
5. Chill until serving. This salad is best eaten the same day, but leftovers can be enjoyed the following day.
6. Serve as a side dish or with tortilla chips as a snack or appetizer.

Hadley's Favorite Vegan Lemon Blueberry Pound Cake

~~~

Ingredients:

<u>Pound Cake</u>
1/2 cup almond flour
1/2 cup oat flour
1 & 1/8 cup whole grain pastry flour
1 teaspoon salt
1/2 cup raw cane sugar
3 teaspoons corn starch
1/4 cup lemon zest
1/2 cup fresh squeezed lemon juice
1/2 cup plant-based butter (I use MiYoko's European style)
1/3 cup plant-based cream cheese (I use MiYoko's)
1/2 cup cashew milk
1/3 cup plant-based yogurt
2 cups blueberries

<u>Lemon Glaze</u>
1 cup powdered sugar
3 tablespoons fresh squeezed lemon juice

Directions:

1. Preheat the oven to 425.
2. In a large mixing bowl, combine the almond flour, oat flour, whole grain pastry flour, salt, sugar, and cornstarch. Mix well.
3. Add lemon zest to the dry ingredients mixture.
4. In a medium-sized bowl, combine the lemon juice, melted butter, cream cheese, cashew milk, and plant-based yogurt. Mix well.
5. Mix the wet ingredients with the dry ingredients, and mix well.
6. Toss 1 & 1/2 cups blueberries with 2 tablespoons whole grain pastry flour. This step keeps the blueberries evenly distributed in the cake.
7. Add the blueberries to the batter.
8. Grease a silicone Bundt pan with plant-based butter and lightly coat with flour. Pour the batter into the pan. Place in the oven and bake for 50 minutes.
9. In a separate bowl, mix 1 cup powered sugar with 3 tablespoons fresh lemon juice to make the glaze. If the consistency isn't to your preference, add additional lemon juice one tablespoon at a time.
10. Drizzle glaze over cake, garnish with remaining 1/2 cup blueberries, and enjoy.

Libba's Carolina Shrimp Salad

Ingredients:

Marinade
¼ cup fresh squeezed lemon juice
⅛ cup extra virgin olive oil
2 tablespoons freshly minced garlic
1 teaspoon Old Bay Seasoning
1 teaspoon salt
1 tablespoon Worcestershire Sauce
1 tablespoon honey
2 pounds shrimp (fresh if you can get them—frozen works fine otherwise) *

Salad
Butter lettuce for six dinner size salads (we like Organic Girl Butter Plus)
6 hard boiled eggs, halved
1 pound cherry tomatoes, halved
½ English cucumber, diced (more or less to taste)
2 large ripe avocados, diced
Capers, drained

Flaky salt
Fresh ground black pepper

<u>Dressing</u>
2 cups Duke's mayonnaise
¼ cup red chili sauce
¼ cup sweet chili sauce
2 tablespoons fresh squeezed lemon juice
2 tablespoons chopped onion
1 tablespoon dijon mustard
1 tablespoon Worcestershire Sauce
1 teaspoon horseradish
4 tablespoons capers, drained
2 teaspoons fresh minced garlic
½ teaspoon smoked paprika

* Sometimes we marinate and grill the shrimp, and sometimes we opt for simplicity and buy large, cooked shrimp at The Fresh Market. We really like shrimp, and good shrimp doesn't really need a marinade—unless, of course, you're in the mood, as we sometimes are.

Note: This recipe serves about six people who like shrimp. If your group isn't filled with shrimp enthusiasts like mine, and you only have four mouths to feed, you could halve everything and be fine. I'm just not personally able to feed four mouths with one pound of shrimp unless two have gone vegan temporarily.

Directions:

1. Whip up the dressing the day before if time allows. It's better after the flavors marry. Add everything except the capers to a high speed blender and blend until smooth. Then stir in the capers. Chill until ready to serve.

2. If using frozen shrimp, thaw according to package directions. Peel and devein if necessary.
3. Whisk together marinade ingredients in a large bowl.
4. Add shrimp and toss to evenly coat.
5. Move to refrigerator and marinate for no more than 30 minutes. (Marinating shrimp longer can make it mushy).
6. Divide the salad ingredients among six plates and chill if you have the refrigerator space.
7. Grill shrimp on medium-hot grill (400°) until pink, about 2-3 minutes per side. Be careful not to overcook. (It's so easy to overcook shrimp, isn't it?)
8. If you need a quicker method, sauté the shrimp in a cast iron pan with a bit of olive oil.
9. Remove shrimp to a plate and chill for at least thirty minutes.
10. When ready to serve, sprinkle flaky salt on the eggs, give the salads a twist or two of fresh ground pepper, scatter shrimp on the salads, and top with dressing.

Tallulah's Fettuccine Alfredo

Ingredients:

4 cups heavy cream
8 ounces (2 sticks) unsalted butter (I like Plugra)
4 cups grated Parmigiano-Reggiano cheese
⅛ teaspoon freshly grated nutmeg
Salt and freshly ground pepper, to taste
2 pounds fresh fettuccine
1 tablespoon sea salt

Directions:

1. In a large saucepan bring the cream and butter to a boil over medium-high heat.
2. Lower heat to a simmer and cook about a minute.
3. Gradually add half the grated cheese, whisking until smooth.
4. Remove from the heat and add the nutmeg and pepper. Taste before you add salt, then gradually add more, tasting as you go, until you have the desired

amount of salt. It's easy to get too much in combination with the parmesan cheese.

5. Bring a large pot of water to boil over high heat.
6. Add the sea salt and fresh pasta and cook until it reaches the desired tenderness, about 3 minutes.
7. Drain well.
8. Add pasta to one or two large, warmed pasta bowls. Depending on bowl size, one may be enough but two may be necessary. I warm the bowls ahead of time with water from the tea kettle.
9. Pour on the sauce, sprinkle with the remaining cheese and toss well.
10. Serve immediately with additional cheese and black pepper.

Note: This is a simple recipe. It's all about the quality of the ingredients. I only make it for special occasions because it's quite rich. When I do make it, I buy fresh pasta from a local shop and splurge on the cream, butter, and cheese. This recipe makes eight generous entrée servings or twelve first course servings. It can easily be halved for more intimate gatherings.

About the Author

Susan M. Boyer is the *USA Today* bestselling author of thirteen novels. Her debut novel, *Lowcountry Boil*, won the 2012 Agatha Award for Best First Novel, the Daphne du Maurier Award for Excellence in Mystery/Suspense, and garnered several other award nominations. Subsequent books in the Liz Talbot Mystery Series have been nominated for various honors, including Southern Independent Booksellers Alliance Okra Picks, the 2016 Pat Conroy Beach Music Mystery Prize, and the 2017 Southern Book Prize in Mystery & Detective Fiction.

Big Trouble on Sullivan's Island, the first novel in her Carolina Tales series, won the 2024 Independent Publisher Book Award silver medal in Southeast Regional Fiction and was a 2024 National Indie Excellence Award finalist.

Susan is a lifelong Carolinian. She grew up in a small North Carolina town and has lived most of her life in South Carolina. She loves beaches, Southern food, and small towns where everyone knows everyone, and everyone has crazy relatives. You'll find all of the above in her novels. She and her husband call Greenville, South Carolina, home and spend as much time as possible on the Carolina coast.

If you'd like to be among the first to hear about new releases, events, and sales, sign up for Susan's newsletter on any page of her website by scrolling to the bottom or waiting for the pop-up.

susanmboyer.com

Sunsplashed Southern Stories

BY SUSAN M. BOYER

Carolina Tales Series

Big Trouble on Sullivan's Island

Beginnings - The Sullivan's Island Supper Club (Prequel)

The Sullivan's Island Supper Club

Trouble's Turn to Lose (April 8, 2025)

Hard Candy Christmas (October 28, 2025)

The Liz Talbot Series

Lowcountry Boil (A Liz Talbot Mystery # 1)

Lowcountry Bombshell (A Liz Talbot Mystery # 2)

Lowcountry Boneyard (A Liz Talbot Mystery # 3)

Postcards From Stella Maris (Five Liz Talbot Short Stories)

Lowcountry Bordello (A Liz Talbot Mystery # 4)

Lowcountry Book Club (A Liz Talbot Mystery # 5)

Lowcountry Bonfire (A Liz Talbot Mystery # 6)

Lowcountry Bookshop (A Liz Talbot Mystery # 7)

Lowcountry Boomerang (A Liz Talbot Mystery # 8)

Lowcountry Boondoggle (A Liz Talbot Mystery # 9)

Lowcountry Boughs of Holly (A Liz Talbot Mystery # 10)

Lowcountry Getaway (A Liz Talbot Mystery # 11)

Made in the USA
Las Vegas, NV
12 September 2024

95193221R00052